Let's Be Honest

P. K. Hallinan

ideals children's books®

Nashville, Tennessee

ISBN-13: 978-0-8249-5580-9

Published by Ideals Children's Books
An imprint of Ideals Publications
A Guideposts Company
Nashville, Tennessee
www.idealsbooks.com

Color separations by Precision Color Graphics, Franklin, Wisconsin
Printed and bound in the United States of America

Library of Congress Cataloging-in-Publication Data

Hallinan. P.K.
  Let's be honest / P.K. Hallinan.
      p. cm.
Summary: Introduces the concept of honesty as a young child describes
why it is best to tell the truth at all times.
(alk. paper)
 [1. Honesty--Fiction. 2. Stories in rhyme.] I. Title: Let us be honest. II.
Title.
PZ8.3.H15Lc 2003
 [E]--dc22

                                    2003025176

Designed by Georgina Chidlow-Rucker

10 9 8 7 6 5 4 3 2

This book is for

_____

◆ ◆ ◆

From

_____

I try to be honest in every way,
From the things that I do

To the things that I say!

When I'm honest with others,
It's easy to see,
They tend to be friendly
And honest with me.

Sometimes I'll make a little mistake.

Or I'll tell a tall tale . . .

Or I'll hide what I break.

But whenever I say
What I know isn't true . . .

I feel kind of lonely,
Unhappy, and blue!

But then, when I'm honest,
It's a marvelous thing . . .

I feel so much better
My heart starts to sing!

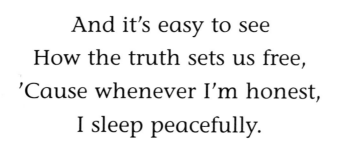

And it's easy to see
How the truth sets us free,
'Cause whenever I'm honest,
I sleep peacefully.

Sometimes I'll worry that something I've done
Is just too upsetting to tell anyone.

But then when I do, it's amazingly clear,
I'm always forgiven—and my fears disappear!

Of course, there are times
That I don't speak my mind,
For words that hurt others
Are best left behind.

Yes, I like to be honest in every way.
It lightens my life, and it brightens my day!

And whenever I'm wondering what to say or to do,
The answer is always . . .

Just be honest and true!